ROBERT LOUIS STEVENSON'S

Treasure Island

THE GRAPHIC NOVEL

adapted by
Tim Hamilton

PUFFIN BOOKS

PUFFIN BOOKS
Published by the Penguin Group
Penguin Young Readers Group,
345 Hudson Street, New York, NY 10014 U.S.A.
Penguin Group (Canada), 10 Alcorn Avenue, Toronto, Ontario, Canada M4V 3B2
(a division of Pearson Penguin Canada Inc.)
Penguin Books Ltd, 80 Strand, London WC2R 0RL, England
Penguin Ireland, 25 St. Stephen's Green, Dublin 2, Ireland
(a division of Penguin Books Ltd)
Penguin Group (Australia), 250 Camberwell Road, Camberwell, Victoria 3124,
Australia (a division of Pearson Australia Group Pty Ltd)
Penguin Books India Pvt Ltd, 11 Community Centre, Panchsheel Park,
New Delhi – 110 017, India
Penguin Group (NZ), Cnr Airborne and Rosedale Roads, Albany, Auckland 1310,
New Zealand (a division of Pearson New Zealand Ltd)
Penguin Books (South Africa) (Pty) Ltd, 24 Sturdee Avenue, Rosebank,
Johannesburg 2196, South Africa

Registered Offices: Penguin Books Ltd, 80 Strand, London WC2R 0RL, England

First published by Puffin Books, a division of Penguin Young Readers Group, 2005

10 9 8 7 6 5 4 3 2 1

A Byron Preiss Book
Byron Preiss Visual Publications
24 West 25th Street, New York, NY 10010

Adapted by Tim Hamilton
Cover art by Tim Hamilton
Series Editor: Dwight Jon Zimmerman
Series Assistant Editor: April Isaacs
Interior design by Matt Postawa, Raul Carvajal and Gilda Hannah
Cover design by Matt Postawa

Puffin Books ISBN 0-14-240470-5

Printed in the United States of America

ROBERT LOUIS STEVENSON'S

Treasure Island

SQUIRE TRELAWNEY, DR. LIVESEY, AND THE REST OF THE *GENTLEMEN* HAVING ASKED ME TO WRITE DOWN THE PARTICULARS ABOUT *TREASURE ISLAND*, FROM BEGINNING TO END, I TAKE UP THE *PEN*...

...AND GO BACK TO THE TIME WHEN MY FATHER KEPT THE *ADMIRAL BENBOW INN,* AND THE BROWN OLD *SEAMAN*, WITH THE SABER CUT, FIRST TOOK UP LODGINGS UNDER OUR ROOF.

I *REMEMBER* HIM AS IF IT WAS YESTERDAY...

8

WHEN A SEAMAN PUT UP AT THE *ADMIRAL BENBOW*, HE WAS ALWAYS SURE TO BE AS *SILENT* AS A MOUSE WHEN ANY SUCH WAS *PRESENT*.

FOR ME, AT LEAST, THERE WAS NO *SECRET* ABOUT THE MATTER; FOR I WAS, IN A WAY, A *SHARER* IN HIS *ALARMS*.

HE HAD PROMISED ME A *SILVER FOURPENNY* ON THE FIRST OF EVERY MONTH IF I WOULD ONLY KEEP MY "WEATHER-EYE OPEN FOR A *SEAFARING MAN* WITH ONE LEG."

AND LET HIM KNOW THE *MOMENT* HE APPEARED.

11

TO SEE HIM *PURSUE* ME OVER HEDGE AND DITCH WAS THE WORST OF *NIGHTMARES.*

I PAID *PRETTY DEAR* FOR MY MONTHLY FOURPENNY PIECE, IN THE SHAPE OF THESE *ABOMINABLE FANCIES.*

BUT THOUGH I WAS SO TERRIFIED BY THE IDEA OF THE SEAFARING MAN WITH ONE *LEG...*

I WAS FAR *LESS AFRAID* OF THE *CAPTAIN* HIMSELF THAN ANYBODY ELSE WHO *KNEW* HIM.

HIS *STORIES* WERE WHAT FRIGHTENED PEOPLE MOST OF ALL. MY *FATHER* WAS ALWAYS SAYING THE INN WOULD BE *RUINED.*

PEOPLE WERE *FRIGHTENED* AT THE TIME, BUT ON LOOKING BACK, THEY RATHER *LIKED* IT; IT WAS A FINE *EXCITEMENT* IN A QUIET COUNTRY LIFE.

HE WAS ONLY ONCE *CROSSED,* AND THAT WAS TOWARDS THE *END.*

WHEN MY POOR *FATHER* WAS FAR GONE IN A *DECLINE.*

14

15

16

IT WAS NOT VERY LONG AFTER THIS THAT THERE OCCURRED THE FIRST OF THE *MYSTERIOUS EVENTS* THAT RID US OF THE CAPTAIN, THOUGH NOT OF HIS AFFAIRS.

WINTER ARRIVED BITTER COLD, AND MY POOR *FATHER* SEEMED UNLIKELY TO SEE SPRING AS HE FELL MORE INTO *ILLNESS*.

THEN, ONE JANUARY MORNING...

IS THIS HERE TABLE FOR MY MATE, *BILL*?

22

25

PROBABLY I SHOULD HAVE *TOLD* THE WHOLE *STORY* TO THE DOCTOR. BUT AS THINGS FELL OUT, MY POOR FATHER *DIED* QUITE SUDDENLY THAT EVENING.

AFTER THAT, I WAS SO *BUSY* THAT I HAD SCARCELY TIME TO *THINK* OF THE CAPTAIN, FAR LESS TO BE *AFRAID* OF HIM.

BUT, HE MINDED PEOPLE LESS, AND SEEMED SHUT UP IN HIS OWN THOUGHTS.

THE CAPTAIN HAD AN ALARMING WAY NOW...OF DRAWING HIS CUTLASS AND LAYING IT BARE BEFORE HIM.

TEN O'CLOCK! GIVES US *SIX HOURS.* WE'LL DO THEM *YET.*

SUDDENLY, HE *REELED,* PUT HIS HAND TO HIS *THROAT,* AND THEN *FELL.*

THE CAPTAIN HAD BEEN STRUCK *DEAD* BY THUNDERING *APOPLEXY.*

TAP
TAP
TAP

I LOST NO TIME IN TELLING MY MOTHER ALL THAT I KNEW. WE SAW OURSELVES AT ONCE IN A DIFFICULT AND DANGEROUS POSITION.

IT SEEMED IMPOSSIBLE FOR EITHER OF US TO REMAIN MUCH LONGER IN THE *HOUSE.* IT OCCURRED TO US TO GO FORTH TOGETHER AND SEEK HELP IN THE NEIGHBORING HAMLET.

WHAT GREATLY ENCOURAGED ME WAS THAT IT WAS IN AN *OPPOSITE DIRECTION* FROM THAT WHENCE THE BLIND MAN HAD MADE HIS APPEARANCE.

IT WAS ALREADY *CANDLE-LIGHT* WHEN WE REACHED THE HAMLET.

BUT NO SOUL WOULD CONSENT TO *RETURN* WITH US TO THE ADMIRAL BENBOW. THE MORE WE TOLD OF OUR *TROUBLES*, THE MORE, MAN, WOMAN, AND CHILD, THEY CLUNG TO THE SHELTER OF THEIR HOUSES.

THE NAME OF *CAPTAIN FLINT*, THOUGH IT WAS STRANGE TO ME, WAS WELL ENOUGH KNOWN TO SOME THERE, AND CARRIED A GREAT WEIGHT OF TERROR.

WHILE WE COULD GET *SEVERAL* WHO WERE WILLING ENOUGH TO RIDE TO DR. LIVESEY'S...

...WHICH LAY IN ANOTHER DIRECTION, NONE WOULD *HELP* US TO DEFEND THE INN.

ALL THEY WOULD DO WAS TO GIVE ME A *LOADED PISTOL,* AND TO PROMISE TO HAVE *HORSES* READY SADDLED, IN CASE WE WERE *PURSUED.*

MY *HEART* WAS BEATING FINELY WHEN WE TWO SET FORTH *BACK* TO THE ADMIRAL BENBOW.

WE HAVE TO GET THE *KEY* OFF THAT!

PERHAPS IT'S ROUND HIS *NECK.*

AFTER WE FOUND THE KEY, WE HURRIED *UPSTAIRS.*

GIVE ME THE *KEY.*

35

TAP TAP TAP TAP TAP TAP TAP TAP TAP TAP

TAP TAP TAP TAP TAP TAP TAP TAP TAP TAP

38

39

40

I LEAPED TO MY FEET AND *HAILED* THE RIDERS. THEY WERE *REVENUE OFFICERS* AND TO THEM MY MOTHER AND I OWED OUR *PRESERVATION* FROM DEATH.

THEY GOT OFF *CLEAN*, AND THERE'S AN END.

PEW WAS DEAD, *STONE DEAD.* BUT HIS MATES MADE IT TO THEIR *LUGGER* IN KIT'S HOLE AND *ESCAPED.* REVENUE SUPERVISOR DANCE SAID HE STOOD "LIKE A FISH OUT OF WATER" AS HE WATCHED THE SHIP DISAPPEAR.

"I MIGHT AS WELL *ROUND THERE* MYSELF," HE SAID. "HAWKINS, I'LL TAKE YOU ALONG. DOGGER, YOU HAVE A GOOD HORSE, TAKE UP THIS LAD *BEHIND* YOU."

WE FOUND DR. LIVESEY AT THE HOME OF *SQUIRE TRELAWNEY.*

IT WAS THERE THAT WE *TOLD* WHAT HAD OCCURRED. I GAVE DR. LIVESEY THE CAPTAIN'S *OILSKIN PACKET.*

"YOU HAVE *HEARD* OF THIS *FLINT*, SQUIRE?" ASKED DR. LIVESEY.

HE WAS THE *BLOODTHIRSTIEST* BUCCANEER THAT SAILED.

HMMMM. "BULK OF TREASURE *HERE.*"

LIVESEY, IN THREE WEEK'S TIME, WE'LL HAVE THE *BEST SHIP* IN SEARCH OF THAT SPOT.

IT WAS LONGER THAN THE SQUIRE IMAGINED ERE WE WERE *READY* FOR THE SEA. I RECEIVED A *LETTER* DATED MARCH 1, FROM SQUIRE TRELAWNEY.

"THE *SHIP* IS BOUGHT AND FITTED. SHE LIES AT ANCHOR, READY FOR SEA. NAME: *HISPANIOLA.*

"WITH THE *CREW*, I HAD THE MOST REMARKABLE STROKE OF FORTUNE. *LONG JOHN SILVER*, WHO LOST A LEG IN HIS COUNTRY'S SERVICE, I ENGAGED AS A *COOK.* THANKS TO HIM, I NOW HAVE A *CREW.*

"COME FULL SPEED TO *BRISTOL.*"

I SAID *GOODBYE* TO MOTHER AND THE ADMIRAL BENBOW, AND A FEW DAYS *LATER* I ARRIVED IN BRISTOL.

47

48

AND NOW, JIM MAY COME *ON BOARD* WITH US, MAY HE NOT?

TO BE SURE HE *MAY.*

TAKE YOUR *HAT,* HAWKINS, AND WE'LL *SEE* THE SHIP.

THE *HISPANIOLA* LAY SOME WAY OUT, AND WE WENT UNDER THE *FIGUREHEADS* AND ROUND THE STERNS OF MANY OTHER SHIPS.

AT LAST, HOWEVER, WE GOT *ALONGSIDE*. I SOON OBSERVED THAT THINGS WERE *NOT FRIENDLY* BETWEEN MR. TRELAWNEY AND THE CAPTAIN.

WELL, *CAPTAIN SMOLLETT*, ALL WELL, I HOPE. ALL *SHIPSHAPE* AND SEAWORTHY?

WELL, SIR, BETTER SPEAK *PLAIN*.

I *DON'T LIKE* THIS CRUISE. I DON'T LIKE THE *MEN*. AND I DON'T LIKE MY OFFICER.

51

I AM *RESPONSIBLE* FOR THE SHIP'S *SAFETY.*

I ASK YOU TO TAKE CERTAIN *PRECAUTIONS.* AND YOU'LL FIND I DO MY *DUTY.*

A LITTLE BEFORE *DAWN,* THE BOATSWAIN SOUNDED HIS *PIPE,* AND THE CREW BEGAN TO MAN THE *CAPSTAINS.*

ALL WAS SO *NEW* AND INTERESTING TO ME...THE BRIEF *COMMANDS,* THE SHRILL NOTE OF THE *WHISTLE,* THE MEN BUSTLING TO THEIR PLACES IN THE *GLIMMER* OF THE SHIP'S LANTERNS.

FIFTEEN MEN ON THE *DEAD MAN'S CHEST...*

YO-HO-HO, AND A BOTTLE OF RUM!

I AM NOT GOING TO RELATE THAT *VOYAGE* IN DETAIL.

THE SHIP PROVED TO BE A *GOOD SHIP.*

THE CREW WERE *CAPABLE SEAMEN.*

AND THE CAPTAIN THOROUGHLY *UNDERSTOOD* HIS BUSINESS.

BUT THE *ONE MAN* ALL THE CREW RESPECTED AND EVEN *OBEYED* WAS *LONG JOHN SILVER.*

TO ME HE WAS UNWEARIEDLY *KIND;* AND ALWAYS GLAD TO SEE ME IN THE *GALLEY.*

THERE WAS A GREAT *RUSH* OF FEET ACROSS THE *DECK.*

SLIPPING IN AN INSTANT OUTSIDE MY *BARREL,* I DIVED BEHIND THE FORE-SAIL AND MADE A DOUBLE TOWARDS THE *STERN.*

I CAME OUT UPON THE OPEN DECK IN TIME TO JOIN *DR. LIVESEY* IN THE RUSH FOR THE BOW.

DR. LIVESEY CALLED ME TO HIS SIDE. AS SOON AS I WAS NEAR ENOUGH TO *SPEAK* AND NOT BE *OVERHEARD,* I SAID...

DOCTOR, GET THE CAPTAIN AND SQUIRE DOWN TO THE *CABIN,* AND THEN MAKE SOME *PRETENSE* TO SEND FOR ME.

I HAVE *TERRIBLE NEWS.*

NOT LONG AFTER...

I DID AND, AS *SHORT* AS I COULD MAKE IT, TOLD THE WHOLE *DETAILS* OF SILVER'S CONVERSATION.

NOW, HAWKINS, *SPEAK UP.*

CAPTAIN, YOU WERE RIGHT, AND I WAS *WRONG.* I AWAIT YOUR *ORDERS.*

WE MUST *GO ON.* IF I GAVE THE WORD TO GO ABOUT, THEY WOULD *RISE* AT ONCE. THE *BEST* THAT I CAN SAY IS *NOT MUCH.*

WE MUST KEEP A *BRIGHT LOOK-OUT* UNTIL WE KNOW WHO IN THE CREW WE CAN *TRUST.*

JIM CAN *HELP* US MORE THAN ANYONE. THE MEN ARE NOT *SHY* WITH HIM.

WE BROUGHT UP WITH *TREASURE ISLAND* ON ONE SIDE, AND *SKELETON ISLAND* ON THE OTHER.

MUTINY, IT WAS PLAIN, HUNG OVER US LIKE A THUNDER-CLOUD.

AND NOT ONLY WE PERCEIVED THE *DANGER.*

SILVER IS ANXIOUS TO TALK THEM *OUT* OF IT. I PROPOSE TO GIVE HIM THE *CHANCE.*

MY LADS! WE ARE ALL *TIRED* AND OUT OF SORTS.

A TURN ASHORE'LL HURT NOBODY. YOU CAN TAKE THE *GIGS*, AND AS MANY AS PLEASE CAN GO ASHORE FOR THE *AFTERNOON*.

I'LL FIRE A GUN HALF AN HOUR BEFORE *SUNDOWN*.

THE CREW ALL CAME OUT OF THEIR *SULKS* IN A MOMENT, AND GAVE A *CHEER* THAT STARTED THE ECHO IN A FAR-AWAY HILLL.

THE CAPTAIN LEFT SILVER TO *ARRANGE* THE PARTY. *SIX FELLOWS* WERE TO STAY ON BOARD, AND THE REMAINING *THIRTEEN*, INCLUDING SILVER, BEGAN TO *EMBARK*.

IT WAS THEN THAT IT CAME INTO MY HEAD THE FIRST OF THE *MAD NOTIONS* THAT CONTRIBUTED SO MUCH TO *SAVE* OUR LIVES.

IT WAS *PLAIN* THAT THE CABIN PARTY HAD NO PRESENT *NEED* OF MY ASSISTANCE. IT OCCURRED TO ME AT ONCE TO GO *ASHORE.*

IN A JIFFY I HAD SLIPPED OVER THE *SIDE,* AND CURLED UP IN THE FORESHEETS OF THE *NEAREST BOAT* ALMOST AT THE SAME MOMENT SHE *SHOVED OFF.*

IS THAT YOU, JIM? KEEP YOUR HEAD *DOWN.*

THE CREWS *RACED* FOR THE BEACH.

THE BOAT I WAS IN SHOT FAR *AHEAD.*

I CAUGHT A *BRANCH* AND SWUNG MYSELF OUT, AND PLUNGED INTO THE NEAREST *THICKET* WHILE SILVER AND THE REST WERE *BEHIND.*

SOON I HEARD THE LOW TONES OF A *HUMAN VOICE.*

I CRAWLED *UNDER COVER* OF THE NEAREST LIVE-OAK, AND SQUATTED THERE, HEARKENING, AS *SILENT* AS A MOUSE.

CRAWLING ON ALL FOURS, I MADE *SLOWLY* TOWARDS THEM WHERE I COULD SEE *LONG JOHN SILVER* AND...

YOU'VE *KILLED* ALAN, HAVE YOU? KILL ME, TOO, IF YOU CAN. BUT I *DEFIES* YOU.

PRESENTLY I BEGAN TO FEEL THAT I WAS *NEGLECTING* MY BUSINESS; THAT SINCE I HAD COME ASHORE, THE LEAST I COULD DO WAS TO *OVERHEAR* THEM.

URKK

I BEGAN TO *EXTRICATE* MYSELF AND CRAWL BACK AGAIN, WITH WHAT *SPEED* AND *SILENCE* I COULD MANAGE.

AS I DID SO, I COULD HEAR *HAILS* COMING AND GOING BETWEEN THE *OLD BUCCANEER* AND HIS COMRADES, AND THIS SOUND OF *DANGER* LENT ME WINGS.

IT WAS ALL *OVER*, I THOUGHT. GOODBY TO THE *HISPANIOLA;* GOODBYE TO THE SQUIRE, THE DOCTOR, AND THE CAPTAIN!

THERE WAS *NOTHING* LEFT FOR ME BUT *DEATH* BY STARVATION, OR DEATH BY THE HANDS OF THE *MUTINEERS.*

AND THEN A *FRESH ALARM* BROUGHT ME TO A *STANDSTILL* WITH A THUMPING HEART.

MEANWHILE, ON THE *HISPANIOLA*...

MR. HANDS.

HERE ARE TWO OF US WITH A BRACE OF *PISTOLS* EACH. IF ANY ONE OF YOU SIX MAKE A *SIGNAL* OF ANY DESCRIPTION WHILE WE SEND *SUPPLIES* ASHORE...

...THAT MAN'S *DEAD*.

71

72

I WAS IN *ANOTHER SHIP* THREE YEARS BACK, AND WE *SIGHTED* THIS ISLAND.

"BOYS," I SAID, "HERE'S *FLINT'S TREASURE;* LET'S LAND AND FIND IT."

THE CAP'N WAS *DISPLEASED;* BUT MY MESSMATES WERE ALL OF A MIND, AND *LANDED.*

TWELVE DAYS THEY LOOKED FOR IT, AND EVERY DAY THEY HAD THE *WORSE WORD* FOR ME UNTIL ONE FINE MORNING *ALL HANDS* WENT ABOARD.

"AS FOR *YOU,* BENJAMIN GUNN. YOU CAN *STAY HERE,* AND FIND FLINT'S MONEY FOR YOURSELF," THEY SAYS.

K-BOOM K-BOOM

THEY HAVE BEGUN TO *FIGHT!* FOLLOW ME!

76

SP-WSSH

HUNTER RUSHED FROM THE **STOCKADE** TO HELP THEM.

MAKE YOUR **BEST SPEED!**

THE **VOICES** OF THE BUCCANEERS RANG NEARER, AS DID THE **SOUNDS** OF THEIR FOOTFALLS AS THEY RAN.

THEN, AT THE **EDGE** OF THE WOOD AND NEAR THE **STOCKADE...**

K-POW

K-POW

UNH!

K-BAM

TOM!

81

82

"WHEN THEY ASKED ABOUT THE *TREASURE*, HE TOLD THEM THEY WERE FREE TO GO ASHORE...

"BEN GUNN LATER WAS ON *ANOTHER SHIP* THAT CAME ACROSS THIS ISLAND.

"...BUT THE SHIP WAS OFF FOR MORE *PLUNDERING*.

"HE CONVINCED THE *CREW* TO GO ASHORE TO FIND THE TREASURE. WHEN THEY DIDN'T, THEY *LEFT* HIM BEHIND.

"HE IS VERY *CONCERNED* ABOUT THE FACT THAT *SILVER* AND HIS MEN ARE ON THE ISLAND.

"HE WANTS TO MEET WITH *YOU* AND MAKE A *SQUARE DEAL*."

90

91

ROUND THE HOUSE, LADS! *ROUND* THE HOUSE!

MECHANICALLY I *OBEYED*.

NEXT *MOMENT* I WAS FACE TO FACE WITH ANDERSON.

I HAD NOT TIME TO BE *AFRAID*.

THUNK

THE *MUTINEERS* HAD BEEN READY TO MAKE AN END OF US. AND YET, IN A SHORT BREATH OF *TIME*...

...THE FIGHT WAS *OVER*.

THE *VICTORY* WAS OURS.

THE CAPTAIN'S *WOUNDED*.

HAVE THEY RUN?

ALL THAT *COULD*. BUT FIVE WILL NEVER RUN AGAIN.

THE CAPTAIN'S *WOUNDS* WERE GRIEVOUS, BUT NOT *DANGEROUS.* HE WAS SURE TO *RECOVER,* THE DOCTOR SAID.

AFTER DINNER, THE *DOCTOR* TOOK UP HIS HAT AND PISTOLS...

...CROSSED THE *PALISADE* ON THE NORTH SIDE, AND SET OFF BRISKLY THROUGH THE *TREES.*

IS DR. LIVESEY *MAD?*

WHY, *NO.* HE'S GOING NOW TO SEE *BEN GUNN.*

WITH SO MUCH *BLOOD* ABOUT ME, I TOOK A *DISGUST* OF THE PLACE THAT WAS ALMOST AS STRONG AS *FEAR.*

I WAS A *FOOL*, IF YOU LIKE, AND CERTAINLY I WAS GOING TO DO A FOOLISH, *OVER-BOLD ACT.*

BUT I WAS *DETERMINED* TO DO IT WITH ALL THE PRECAUTIONS IN MY POWER.

I DROPPED INTO THE HOLLOW, AND THERE, AS HE HAD TOLD ME, WAS *BEN GUNN'S BOAT,* HOME-MADE IF EVERY ANYTHING WAS HOME-MADE.

MY *NOTION* WAS TO SLIP OUT UNDER COVER OF THE NIGHT, CUT THE *HISPANIOLA ADRIFT,* AND LET HER GO ASHORE WHERE SHE FANCIED.

95

DOWN I SAT TO WAIT FOR *DARKNESS.*

THERE WERE BUT *TWO POINTS* VISIBLE ON THE WHOLE ANCHORAGE.

ONE WAS THE GREAT *FIRE* ON SHORE, BY WHICH THE PIRATES LAY CAROUSING.

THE OTHER, THE *ANCHORED SHIP.*

ONE *CUT* WITH MY SEA-GULLY, AND THE *HISPANIOLA* WOULD GO HUMMING DOWN THE *TIDE.*

I HEARD THE SOUND OF *LOUD VOICES* FROM THE CABIN.

I WAS THINKING HOW BUSY DRINK AND THE DEVIL WERE IN THE CABIN OF THE HISPANIOLA, WHEN I WAS SURPRISED BY A SUDDEN LURCH OF THE CORACLE.

ALL AROUND ME WERE LITTLE *RIPPLES*.

BEHIND ME WAS THE *GLOW* OF THE CAMP FIRE.

THE CORACLE HEADED FOR THE *OPEN SEA*.

I DEVOUTLY RECOMMENDED MY *SPIRIT* TO ITS MAKER.

I THOUGHT I MUST FALL INTO SOME BARRAGING BREAKERS, WHERE ALL MY TROUBLES WOULD BE ENDED SPEEDILY.

THOUGH I COULD, PERHAPS, BEAR TO *DIE*, I COULD NOT BEAR TO *LOOK* UPON MY FATE AS IT APPROACHED. I LAY DOWN.

SLEEP AT LAST SUPERVENED, AND IN MY SEA-TOSSED CORACLE, I *DREAMED* OF HOME AND THE OLD ADMIRAL BENBOW.

IT WAS BROAD *DAY* WHEN I AWOKE, AND FOUND MYSELF TOSSING AT THE SOUTHWEST END OF *TREASURE ISLAND.*

I WAS *SURPRISED* HOW EASILY AND *SECURELY* MY LITTLE BOAT COULD RIDE.

EVERY NOW AND AGAIN I GAVE A *WEAK STROKE* OR TWO TO TURN THE CORACLE TO SHORE.

THEN I BEHELD A *SIGHT* THAT CHANGED THE NATURE OF MY THOUGHTS.

THE *HISPANIOLA!*

TO AND FRO, THE *HISPANIOLA* *SAILED* BY SWOOPS AND DASHES. IT BECAME PLAIN TO ME THAT NOBODY WAS *STEERING*.

I SPRANG TO MY FEET AND *LEAPED*.

NOT A *SOUL* WAS TO BE SEEN.

THEN, THE *MAIN BOOM* SWUNG INBOARD, AND SHOWED ME THE LEE AFTER-DECK.

THERE WAS *RED-CAP* AND ISRAEL HANDS. I FELT SURE THAT THEY HAD *KILLED* EACH OTHER IN THEIR DRUNKEN WRATH

...BRANDY...

MISTER *HANDS?*

AYE...! THAT SWAB, HE'S GOOD AND *DEAD* HE IS. HE WARN'T NO SEAMAN, ANYHOW.

AND WHERE MOUGHT *YOU* HAVE COME FROM?

WE STRUCK OUR *BARGAIN* ON THE SPOT. IN THREE MINUTES I HAD THE *HISPANIOLA* SAILIING EASILY BEFORE THE WIND ALONG THE *COAST* OF TREASURE ISLAND.

I WAS GREATLY ELATED WITH *MY NEW COMMAND,* AND PLEASED WITH THE BRIGHT, SUNSHINY WEATHER AND THESE DIFFERENT PROSPECTS OF THE COAST.

WITH NO *ANCHOR,* WE NEEDED TO HAVE THE SCHOONER *STRANDED* SAFE IN A *SHELTERED PLACE* SO THAT WHEN THE TIME CAME SHE COULD BE GOT OFF AGAIN.

THE SHORES OF THE *NORTH INLET* HAD AN ANCHORAGE THAT WAS *CALM.*

110

I WADED ASHORE IN *GREAT SPIRITS.* I HAD NOTHING NEARER MY FANCY THAN TO GET HOME TO THE *STOCKADE* AND BOAST OF MY *ACHIEVEMENTS.*

SO THINKING, I BEGAN TO SET MY FACE FOR THE *BLOCK-HOUSE.*

AT LAST I *ARRIVED.*

THERE WAS NOT A *SOUL* STIRRING.

I WALKED IN AND...

PIECES OF EIGHT!

PIECES OF EIGHT!

PIECES OF EIGHT!

115

119

120

BUT, DOCTOR, I GOT THE SHIP, PART BY LUCK AND PART BY RISKING. SHE LIES IN NORTH INLET.

THE SHIP!

THERE IS A KIND OF *FATE* IN THIS.

SILVER! A PIECE OF ADVICE.

THE TREASURE. LOOK OUT FOR *SQUALLS* WHEN YOU FIND IT.

RAPIDLY I DESCRIBED TO HIM MY *ADVENTURES*. THEN...

AFTER BREAKFAST, WE LEFT TO FIND THE TREASURE. I WAS HORRIBLY *CAST DOWN*.

I HAD A LINE ABOUT MY *WAIST*. FOR ALL THE WORLD, I WAS LED LIKE A *DANCING BEAR*.

MIRY GROUND AND A MATTED, MARISH *VEGETATION*, GREATLY DELAYED OUR PROGRESS.

THE PARTY SPREAD IN A *FAN SHAPE*.

SILVER AND I FOLLOWED.

FROM TIME TO TIME, I HAD TO LEND HIM A *HAND*, OR HE WOULD HAVE MISSED HIS *FOOTING*.

WHAT WE *FOUND*...

...WAS SOMETHING VERY *DIFFERENT*.

A *HUMAN SKELETON*. I BELIEVE A CHILL STRUCK FOR A MOMENT TO EVERY HEART.

TAKE A *BEARING* ALONG THE LINES OF THEM BONES.

THOUGHT SO. THIS WAS FLINT'S DOING YOU CAN BE SURE. THIS IS ONE OF THE SIX HE KILLED. THIS ONE HE HAULED HERE TO BE A COMPASS.

IT WAS DONE. THE COMPASS READ *EAST/SOUTH-EAST AND BY EAST.*

THEY'RE *LONG BONES,* AND THE HAIR'S BEEN YELLOW. THAT WOULD BE *ALLARDYCE.* YOU MIND ALLARDYCE, TOM MORGAN?

AYE, I MIND HIM. HE OWED ME MONEY AND TOOK MY *KNIFE* ASHORE WITH HIM.

129

134

IT WAS EXTRAORDINARY HOW THEIR *SPIRITS* HAD RETURNED.

NOT LONG AFTER, HEARING NO FURTHER *SOUND,* THEY SHOULDERED THE TOOLS AND SET FORTH AGAIN.

WE SOON FOUND THE NEXT MARKER, A *TALL TREE.*

IT WAS HARD FOR ME TO KEEP UP WITH THE *RAPID PACE* OF THE TREASURE-HUNTERS.

HUZZA, MATES, ALL TOGETHER!

THE FOREMOST BROKE INTO A *RUN*.

SUDDENLY NOT TEN YARDS FURTHER, WE BEHELD THEM *STOP*.

A LOW *CRY* AROSE.

BEFORE US WAS A GREAT *EXCAVATION*, NOT VERY RECENT.

ON ONE OF THE BOARDS I SAW THE NAME *WALRUS*, THE NAME OF FLINT'S *SHIP.*

THE CACHE HAD BEEN FOUND. THE TREASURE WAS *GONE!*

JIM, TAKE *THAT.*

AND STAND BY FOR *TROUBLE.*

137

138

BAM

GEORGE, I RECKON I *SETTLED* YOU.

FORWARD! DOUBLE QUICK, MY LADS.

140

142

THE DOCTOR HAD *WORMED* THIS SECRET FROM HIM.

WHEN HE SAW THE *ANCHORAGE* DESERTED, HE WENT TO SILVER.

HE GAVE HIM THE CHART, WHICH WAS NOW *USELESS.*

AND THE SHIP'S *STORES.*

BEN GUNN'S CAVE WAS WELL SUPPLIED WITH *GOAT'S MEAT* SALTED BY HIMSELF.

FINDING OUT THAT JIM WAS TO BE AMONG THE PIRATES AS THEY MADE THEIR DISAPPOINTING *DISCOVERY,* THE DOCTOR, BEN GUNN, AND GRAY HURRIED TO THE TREE.

144

FOR SEVERAL DAYS WE LOADED THE *TREASURE* ON THE HISPANIOLA. THEN WE RAISED ANCHOR AND *LEFT* THE SURVIVING MUTINEERS. ONE SENT A *SHOT* THROUGH THE MAINSAIL.

WE WERE SO SHORT OF MEN THAT *EVERYONE* HAD TO BEAR A HAND. ONLY CAPTAIN SMOLLETT, STILL RECOVERING FROM HIS *WOUNDS,* WAS SPARED.

IT WAS JUST AT *SUNDOWN* WHEN WE CAST ANCHOR AT A MOST BEAUTIFUL LAND-LOCKED GULF.

THE DOCTOR, THE SQUIRE, AND I WENT TO VISIT THE *TOWN.* WHEN WE RETURNED, BEN GUNN WAS ON DECK *ALONE.*

HE MADE US A *CONFESSION.* SILVER WAS *GONE.* GUNN HAD HELPED HIS *ESCAPE,* ASSURING US HE HAD ONLY DONE SO TO *PRESERVE* OUR LIVES.

THE SEA COOK HAD NOT GONE EMPTY-HANDED. HE REMOVED ONE *SACK* OF COIN WORTH THREE OR FOUR HUNDRED *GUINEAS.*

I THINK WE WERE ALL *PLEASED* TO BE SO CHEAPLY *QUIT* OF LONG JOHN SILVER.

TO MAKE A LONG STORY SHORT, WE MADE A *GOOD CRUISE* HOME. ALL OF US HAD AN AMPLE *SHARE* OF THE TREASURE, AND USED IT WISELY OR *FOOLISHLY,* ACCORDING TO OUR NATURE.

OF SILVER WE HAVE HEARD *NO MORE.*

THAT FORMIDABLE *SEAFARING MAN* WITH ONE LEG HAS AT LAST *GONE* CLEAN OUT OF MY LIFE.

THE MAKING OF

ROBERT LOUIS STEVENSON'S

Treasure Island

"I did look forward, with some intimidation, to creating my own take on the look and feel of this novel."

—Tim Hamilton

TIM HAMILTON TALKS ABOUT
Treasure Island

When Byron Preiss approached me with the offer of adapting and illustrating *Treasure Island* as a graphic novel, it was very much a dream job that appeared right out of the blue. I was once like many other kids who had a fascination with pirate stories and treasure. No pirate story ever seemed as ingeniously put together as Robert Louis Stevenson's *Treasure Island.* Even as an adult I still held an interest in historical subject matter revolving around English sailing ships, the real life stories of Captain Kidd, Blackbeard and New World explorers.

Even though I'm not always comfortable with adapting work that seems perfect in its original form, I did look forward, with some intimidation, to creating my own take on the look and feel of this novel. Other artists have done their verson, and I avoided looking at them while working on mine. In fact, I never saw any of the movie versions of *Treasure Island,* even as a kid. I was busy watching the monster movies!

Though intimidated by adapting *Treasure Island,* I was nevertheless drawn into the process by the strong characters and colorful atmosphere. Each setting—the attack on the Admiral Benbow Inn, the trip on the boat and the adventure on the island—had its own feel that I enjoyed bringing to visual life. I stayed up till 1:00 A.M. many nights illustrating scenes from the book just because it was fun to do. I forgot about the fact that it was a job.

PUFFIN CLASSICS

TREASURE ISLAND

ROBERT LOUIS STEVENSON

Tim adapted his story from this Puffin Classics edition of
Treasure Island.

Treasure Island

CONCEPT SKETCHES

A sailing ship.

Jim Hawkins and Long John Silver

Here are some early cover sketches and designs. This page features a sketch complete with a suggested design with indication for title and credits.

A closeup of a pirate.

This sketch was ultimately picked for the final cover, with some
suggested revisions.

Here is the finished pencil art for the final cover, incorporating revisions. Note the differences between the final sketch, and the starting point on the previous page.

157

HOW TIM WORKED ON
Treasure Island

In creating the art for *Treasure Island* I first looked through various art history books that were appropriate to the subject matter. I ended up gravitating towards Japanese art, as much of that art involves the ocean and nature, and *Treasure Island* takes place mostly on an island and at sea. I also looked at the work of Kathe Kollwitz. Her art depicted the common people often in dark and moody settings, which is how I pictured the Benbow Inn and the poor difficult lives of the pirates.

I also did historical research, as the action of *Treasure Island* takes place in the 1700s. I had to find out what clothing, boats, guns and houses looked like in that time period. I found this info in various places, but the library was the main source of my research.

Because of the many characters in *Treasure Island*, I needed real life models and faces to play the parts in the book. Taking pictures of friends in various lighting made the story all the more interesting to illustrate. When drawing a young man like Jim Hawkins as much as I had to draw him in *Treasure Island*, I needed to see his face from as many different angles as possible.

In laying out the book itself I first drew thumbnails—small sketches of the art with a marker so I could see where all the lights and shadows would be placed. This also helped me figure out how to clearly tell the story. I approach storytelling in a cinematic way, and I take inspiration from film history. I study what movie directors like Alfred Hitchcock and Akira Kurosawa have done and learn what I can from them.

After I finished the thumbnails, I transferred the art to Bristol board and made sure the faces of the various characters looked like who they should be before I inked the art with India ink.

When I inked the pencil art for *Treasure Island,* I used whatever tool I needed to get the look I wanted. I used metal pen nibs, good brushes, old damaged brushes, grease crayon and even a wooden stick I carved myself. After that I scanned the pages into the computer and, using the software Photoshop, added gray tones to the art. I then checked for any mistakes. Then I sent the digital files of the art to the publisher to be lettered and printed.

A *Treasure Island* PAGE
FROM SKETCH TO INKS

A rough sketch of a page.

The same page in finished pencil form. Note the detail added to the faces.

The fully inked page. All that remains now is for the lettering to be added.

A ROGUE'S GALLERY OF MODELS

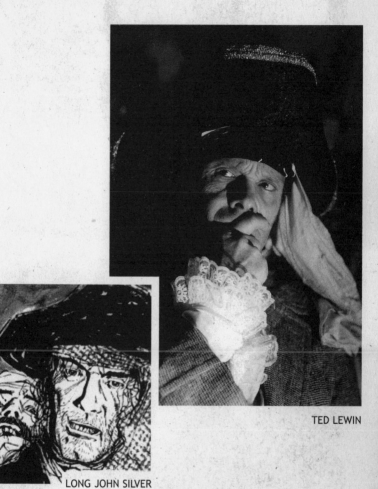

TED LEWIN

LONG JOHN SILVER

As Tim mentioned, he used models for a number of the characters in the story. Here are the real life models and their story counterparts.

AARON BRAUN

JIM HAWKINS

HARVEY WILSON

BILLY BONES

ANDREW DAVENPORT

SQUIRE TRELAWNEY

166

JACOB BRAUN

CAPTAIN SMOLLETT

JIM PORTER

ISRAEL HANDS

Here is a unique opportunity to see the art breakdowns for a scene in a graphic novel. Compare this six-page sequence with the finished art.

ROBERT LOUIS STEVENSON (1850-94) was born into a famous Edinburgh engineering family. His middle name was originally Lewis, but he changed the spelling, while keeping the pronunciation. His father wanted him to study law, and although Robert was called to the Scottish Bar, he made little effort to become successful as a lawyer since he was already trying to make his mark in the world of literature.

While travelling in Europe among somewhat Bohemian circles he met his future wife, an American called Fanny van de Grift Osbourne. She already had a son, Lloyd, by a previous marriage. One day in 1881, Lloyd and his step-father sketched a map of a treasure island, and Lloyd casually said how nice it would be to have a book about it. Fired by the idea, Robert Louis Stevenson created *Treasure Island* and, with his emphasis not just on plot, but also on character, revolutionized the writing of adventure stories. Other famous adventure novels, such as *Kidnapped*, followed, as well as the beautiful *A Child's Garden of Verses*.

TIM HAMILTON began working as an illustrator after graduating from the Art Institute of Pittsburgh in 1987. His first regular assignment illustrating comics was the 1980s comic book series *The Trouble with Girls* written by Gerard Jones. In the 90s Tim worked on a variety of comics including *Aliens* and *Comic's Greatest World* for Dark Horse Comics. At DC Comics he worked on *Justice League Europe*, *Green Lantern*, *Green Lantern Quarterly*, and *Justice League International*. He also illustrated books for Marvel, Malibu, Defiant and Broadway comics. While working for Marvel, Tim created conceptual art involving proposed toys and animated projects for Toybiz. Tim continued his art education at Pratt Institute in the late 90s and now works in New York City as a graphic designer/illustrator. He regularly writes and illustrates humorous comics for *Nickelodeon* Magazine and has produced art for the *New York Times Book Review*, *Cicada*, *King Features* and *Serializer.net*.